PORKCHOP'S HALLOWEEN

BY SUSAN PEARSON
ILLUSTRATED BY RICK BROWN

Simon and Schuster Books for Young Readers
Published by Simon & Schuster Inc. New York

For Rosemary, with love
(and for Porkchop too, of course)

Simon and Schuster Books for Young Readers
Simon & Schuster Building
Rockefeller Center
1230 Avenue of the Americas
New York, New York 10020.

Library of Congress Cataloging-in-Publication Data
Pearson, Susan. Porkchop's Halloween. Sequel to: The day Porkchop climbed the Christmas
tree. Summary: No Halloween has ever been like the one when Rosie is a tube of toothpaste,
her cat Porkchop moves into the pumpkin, and the whole family plays host to a chicken pox
party. [1. Halloween—Fiction. 2. Family life—Fiction. 3. Cats—Fiction] I. Brown, Rick,
1946-   ill.   II. Title. PZ7.P323316Po 1988 [E] 88-4427
ISBN 0-671-66732-7
ISBN 0-671-68872-3 (pbk.)

TABLE OF CONTENTS

CHAPTER 1
PORKCHOP'S COSTUME

My sister, Rosie, has an orange cat named Porkchop.

"He's a Halloween cat," she says. "I chose him because he looks like a pumpkin."

"Then why didn't you name him Pumpkin?" I asked her.

"Lots of people have cats named Pumpkin," she explained. "No one but *me* has a cat named Porkchop."

Halloween is Rosie's favorite holiday. She loves to eat candy. She loves to carve jack-o-lanterns. Most of all, she loves to dress up.

Last year she was a can of soup. The year before she was a carrot. This year she was going to a party.

"Rachel says there's a prize for the best costume," she told me. "I bet I'll win it."

"What are you going to be?" I asked her.

"A tube of toothpaste," said Rosie.

On Saturday, the whole family went to the basement to build the costume. We made the cap from cardboard with holes cut in it so Rosie could see. It looked almost real.

Next Dad shaped some chicken wire into a tube. Mom cut an old sheet to fit around it. Then we painted the sheet.

When it was dry, Mom sewed it all together. Then Rosie tried it on. She looked exactly like a giant toothpaste tube with white arms and purple Reeboks.

Rosie twirled around the kitchen so we could all admire her.

"This is my best costume ever!" she said. "I hope no one else thinks of it."

"I don't think you need to worry about that," said Dad.

Suddenly we heard an awful howl.

"What on earth?" cried Mom.

"It came from the basement," I said.

We all ran downstairs. The black paint can was lying on its side. A black puddle covered the basement floor. Porkchop was standing in the middle of it. He wasn't orange anymore. He was black.

"Oh, no!" Mom groaned.

"What a mess!" said Dad.

"No one but *me* has a cat this smart!" said Rosie. We all stared at her.

"Porkchop made his own costume," she explained. "He's Mr. Tooth Decay."

CHAPTER 2
PORKCHOP'S PUMPKIN

It's too bad no one gives prizes for jack–o–lanterns. Rosie would win those too. Two years ago her pumpkin was the scariest. Last year it was the loudest. Rosie put her radio inside it instead of candles.

"It's a pump rocker," she told us.

This year she wanted the biggest.

She got it. It was so big we almost couldn't get it through the door. We couldn't carry it. We had to slide it up the steps on paper bags. Then we rolled it to the kitchen.

Porkchop must have thought we'd gotten him a giant new ball. He jumped on top of the pumpkin. Then he balanced while we rolled.

"No one but *me* has a circus cat," said Rosie.

The gunk came out of that pumpkin by the barrel. Porkchop loved it. He rolled around in the goo as if it were a field of catnip.

We cut out the pumpkin's eyes, then had to cut them bigger, then had to cut them even bigger to fit the pumpkin's face. Its mouth was as wide as a plate. We traced around the iron to make its nose. When we cut it out, Porkchop jumped inside. He stuck his head out through the hole.

"It will take a candelabra to light this jack-o-lantern!" said Mom.

"She's gorgeous!" said Rosie.

We rolled her to the living room. Porkchop rode inside.

It took all four of us to lift her onto the table in front of the window. On the way up, Porkchop fell out of her nose.

Mom dripped wax and fixed ten candles in her bottom. She lit them. Then we all stood outside and *ooohed* and *aaahed*.

The Turbyfills across the street came outside to admire her. Rosie ran next door to get Rachel. Pretty soon the whole block was standing in our front yard.

"Her name is Glory," said Rosie.

Poor Glory only got lit that once. Late that night, after we were all in bed, Porkchop moved into her. He pushed the candles over and snuggled down inside.

Rosie found him in the morning, sound asleep and purring.

That night she fed Porkchop dinner inside the pumpkin. Then she brought him a towel so his bed would be soft. She pulled the candles out so it wouldn't be lumpy.

"Why don't you just kick him out?" I asked her.

"I couldn't do that," said Rosie. "Porkchop is in love."

CHAPTER 3
PORKCHOP'S PARTY

The Monday before Halloween, Rosie came home from school singing.

"There are five witches in my class," she sang. "Tommy Mason was going to be a tomato, but he has chicken pox. No one but *me* is a toothpaste tube!"

On Tuesday, Rosie reported one ballerina, two pirates, and two witches with chicken pox.

On Wednesday, there were three ghosts, two gypsies, and three more cases of chicken pox. On Thursday, there were four more.

On Friday, Rosie came home from school crying.

"Rachel got them too," she wailed. "No one but *me* doesn't have chicken pox!"

"I thought you liked being different," I said.

"Not this time," said Rosie. "There's no party tomorrow."

We had spaghetti for dinner that night, but Rosie wouldn't eat.

"The Great Pumpkin" was on TV, but Rosie didn't watch.

"Poor kid," said Dad.

"I wish we could do something," said Mom.

"We can!" I said. "I have an idea!"

On Halloween afternoon, Dad went to the dump. He took Rosie and Porkchop with him.

As soon as they left, Mom and I got busy. We hung crepe paper all over the kitchen. We blew up black and orange balloons. Mom made popcorn for popcorn balls. I got out the old washtub and filled it with water. Mom dropped some apples into it. Then we made masks from paper bags. Mom's was a cat face. Mine was a robot. We put them on. Then we turned out the lights and waited.

Pretty soon we heard the garage door open. Then we heard Dad and Rosie coming up the basement stairs. The kitchen light went on.

"Surprise!" we yelled.

"Surprise!" yelled Dad and Rosie at the same time.

"Who's surprising who around here?" Mom asked.

"We're surprising you!" said Rosie. "Look!"

She pointed at her face. There were five red spots—
two on each cheek and one on her nose.

"I got the chicken pox too!" Rosie grinned as wide
as Glory. "I couldn't go to the party now anyway!"

Suddenly Porkchop came racing up the stairs. He stopped short in the doorway. He looked surprised.

He tiptoed over to a balloon. Then he stuck out his paw.

POP!

"It's a party!" shouted Rosie. I guess she hadn't noticed it before.

We made some popcorn balls then, but Porkchop thought they were toys. He chased them all around the kitchen. Then he climbed into my robot mask. Porkchop loves paper bags.

"No one but *me* has a robot cat!" said Rosie.

"Let's bob for apples," said Dad.

"Me first!" I shouted. I'm good at apple bobbing.

I held my breath. Then I plunged my head into the water. I pushed my apple to the side of the tub. I opened my mouth.